Geronimo Stilton
A learned and brainy
mouse; editor of
The Rodent's Gazette

Thea Stilton
Geronimo's sister and
special correspondent at
The Rodent's Gazette

Trap Stilton
An awful joker;
Geronimo's cousin and
owner of the store
Cheap Junk for Less

Benjamin Stilton
A sweet and loving
nine-year-old mouse;
Geronimo's favorite
nephew

Geronimo Stilton

SAVE THE WHITE WHALE!

Scholastic Inc.

New York   Toronto   London   Auckland

Sydney   Mexico City   New Delhi   Hong Kong

ISBN 978-0-545-10377-0

Based on an original idea by Elisabetta Dami.

www.geronimostilton.com

Published by Scholastic Inc., 557 Broadway, New York, NY 10012. SCHOLASTIC and associated logos are trademarks and/or registered trademarks of Scholastic Inc.

Text by Geronimo Stilton
Original title *Salviamo la balena bianca!*
Cover by Giuseppe Ferrario
Illustrations by Sara Copercini (pencils), Riccardo Sisti (ink), and Christian Aliprandi (color)
Graphics by Merenguita Gingermouse and Sara Baruffaldi
Special thanks to Mark Eerdekens and Alessandro Bortolotto

Special thanks to Kathryn Cristaldi
Translated by Lidia Morson Tramontozzi
Interior design by Kay Petronio

19   18 19 20/0

Printed in the U.S.A.   40
First printing, April 2011

SWEATING LIKE A SPRINKLER

It was a SCORCHING summer afternoon.

I was in my office sweating because the air conditioner was broken and . . . Oops, where are my manners? I didn't introduce myself. My name is Stilton, *Geronimo Stilton*. I run *The Rodent's Gazette*, the most popular newspaper on Mouse Island.

Anyway, as I was saying, it was HOT in my office. I tried to get cool by . . .

1. Turning the fans on HURRICANE strength.
2. Wrapping my head in a bandanna packed with ice.
3. Sticking my tail in my minifridge.

Nothing worked. I was still sweating like a sprinkler when I heard a knock at the door. Then the door FLEW open and in walked my friend Petunia Pretty Paws.

Petunia Pretty Paws

YOU SHOULD HAVE
COME WTH ME!

"Hi, G! I was in the neighborhood and thought I'd stop by," Petunia SQUEAKED. "I just got back from an awesome trip to **Antarctica**. I was filming a documentary on penguins. They were so incredibly cool. You should have come with me!"

Here's something you should know about Petunia: She is the most FASCINATING

First Name: Petunia

Last Name: Paws

Nickname: P

Where she lives: She travels all over the world, but her family lives on a farm in Giant Sequoia Valley.

What she does: She's a TV reporter who's always defending the environment, nature, and animals.

What she does in her spare time: She plays the flute and loves to sing and hum songs.

Her secret: She's in love with Geronimo!

rodent I have ever met in my life. She is *pretty* and **smart**, and she **cares deeply** about animals and nature.

Now, here's something else you should know about Petunia: I have a *crush* on her.

Too bad whenever I'm around her, I turn into a bumbling fool. I trip over things and mix up my words. One time I even fell off a ladder when she waved to me.

Some day I'll tell Petunia how much I like her, but for now it's **TOP SECRET!**

Just then I noticed a photo on top of my desk. It was a photo of my cousin Trap, my sister, Thea, and me when we were kids. Every year we'd go on vacation to the **Bay of Whales**.

Suddenly, I had an idea.

"Ahem, Nepunia, I mean, Petunia, I was wondering if you'd like to take a trip with me to the Bay of Whales," I squeaked.

I held my breath. Would she say yes?

"A trip? To the Bay of Whales? I'd love to!" Petunia answered.

I was thrilled. I pictured the two of us lounging on the beach or taking a stroll in the moonlight after dinner.

Maybe I'd even find the courage to tell her how much I liked her.

I was about to tell Petunia more about the Bay of Whales when I realized she was on the phone.

"Bugsy? It's Aunt Patty," she said. "Great news! G invited us to the BEACH! Yes, I'm sure he'll bring Benjamin...."

I bit my tongue. Rats!

How could I tell Petunia I had a crush on

First Name: Bugsy

Last Name: Wugsy

Nickname: Little Tornado

Where she lives: She lives with her father, John Wugsy, and her mother, Furry Paws, on the Paws Farm.

Who she is: She's Petunia Pretty Paws's favorite niece.

Her dream: To become a famous photographer and work with her aunt.

What she does in her spare time: She loves to ride bicycles with her father and to take photographs.

Her secret: She has a crush on Benjamin!

First Name: Benjamin

Last Name: Stilton

Nickname: When he was little, Geronimo always called him his "little morsel of Parmesan cheese."

Where he lives: He lives with Aunt Sweetfur.

Who he is: He's Geronimo's favorite nephew.

His dream: To become a great journalist like his uncle and work with him.

What he does in his spare time: He loves to build historic model planes.

His secret: He doesn't know how to tell jokes, just like his uncle!

her with Bugsy around? Do you know **Bugsy Wugsy**?

She's Petunia's niece, and boy does she live up to her name. She is always bugging me about something.

I closed my eyes. I could just hear her on the beach.

"Uncle G, would you carry my **beach ball**? Uncle G, would you build me a sand castle? Uncle G, would you help me fly a kite?"

Holey cheese . . . I was *exhausted* already!

UNCLE GGGGGGGGGGGGGGGG!

HIGHWAY ROBBERY!

I decided to make the best of it. After all, the Bay of Whales would still be *beautiful* even if Bugsy was there. Plus, I could really use a vacation.

I picked up the phone and called **WHALES AND TAILS BY THE SEA**. I couldn't believe I remembered the number after all these years! Whales and Tails was a charming, SPARKLING CLEAN hotel with a fabumouse view of the bay.

It was run by a kind old lady named Miss Sweetcakes.

A **GRUFF** voice answered the phone.

"Whales and Tails! How many in your

party?" the voice demanded. "Hurry up, I don't have all day!"

I was dumbfounded.

"Is Miss Sweetcakes there? D-d-did something happen to her?" I stammered.

The mouse huffed, "Listen, FURBRAIN, do you want to book a room or what? Come on, make up your mind! Time's ticking!"

What a RUDE mouse. He really needed to work on his phone manners. Maybe I could introduce him to my friend Penelope Perfect Posture. She taught a class on *etiquette* at the New Mouse City College.

For now I said, "My name is Geronimo Stilton and there are four of us. Two adults and two mouselets. I'd like to book this weekend. By the way, HOW MUCH is it per room?"

Um...

For some reason this made the mouse **snicker**. Then he asked me what kind of work I did. When I told him I was the publisher of *The Rodent's Gazette*, he let out a low whistle.

"Publisher? Of the *Gazette*?" he asked. "You must be rolling in dough! For you, every room will cost . . . one thousand dollars a day!"

My eyes **POPPED** out of my head. Well, OK, they didn't *really* pop out of my head, but you get the idea. I was **shocked**.

That was highway robbery!

Still, I didn't want to look like a **cheapskate** in front of Petunia, so I gulped and said, "OK."

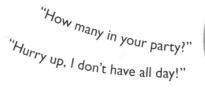

"How many in your party?"
"Hurry up, I don't have all day!"

A SMELLY DUMP!

The next day, Petunia, Bugsy, Benjamin, and I left for the beach. As we were driving, I told Petunia about how beautiful the Bay of Whales was.

But when we got there, I nearly cried. The Bay of Whales was a smelly dump! Ugly GRAY buildings crowded the coastline. And dozens of factories spewed smoke across the sky.

On the beach, papers and garbage littered the sand. And there were so many cars!

"It looks like no one has been taking care of your beautiful beach, G," Petunia fumed. "How could anyone destroy such a NATURAL WONDER?"

We headed for our hotel with **HEAVY** hearts.

From the outside of the building, everything looked just the way I remembered it. . . .

Whales and Tails
by the Sea

Yesterday

WHALES AND TAILS
BY THE SEA

But inside the hotel, things were different. First, Miss Sweetcakes was not at the door. Instead, a gray rat with slicked-back fur and curled whiskers **GLARED** at us from behind the desk. He was wearing a tank top that

looked like it hadn't been washed in months. I noticed a small nameplate on the desk. It read, Phineas Filthyfur: Manager.

I was shocked. How could Miss Sweetcakes hire such a SURLY LOOKING rodent?

"Well, do you have reservations or what?" Phineas squeaked. "I don't have all day!"

I should have known. It was the **RUDE** mouse I had spoken with on the phone.

I stepped up to the desk and was **OVERWHELMED** by the stench of **onions**. **PHEW**! What a stinky rat!

PHINEAS
FILTHYFUR

=

The smell of
ONIONS

"Um, yes, I am Geronimo Stilton. We have a reservation," I said. "But first can you tell me what happened to Miss Sweetcakes?"

Phineas shoved a couple of room keys at me.

"The old lady suffers from asthma because the air is so polluted here. She doesn't run the place anymore. I'm in charge now. Sooner or later, she'll sell it to me," he smirked.

Poor Miss Sweetcakes!

We went up to our rooms. I had room number 13.

We quickly unpacked, put on our bathing suits, and headed out the door for the beach.

But Phineas blocked our way.

"Stop where you are!" he said. "Pay up, or NO SWIMMING!"

I was shocked to hear we had to pay to get on the beach. But I didn't want to look

bad in front of Petunia.

"How much is it?" I asked.

Phineas had a **SNEAKY** smile on his snout.

"That will be two hundred and fifty dollars per rodent!" he squeaked.

I gasped. *HOW OUTRAGEOUS!* But I didn't want to look bad in front of Petunia, so I paid.

Oh, what a miserable vacation!

As soon as we set paw on the beach, a lifeguard with **HUMONGOUS** muscles

$250 dollars + $250 dollars + $250 dollars + $250 dollars = $1,000 dollars!

strode up. He led us to our beach umbrella. Then he stuck out his paw, waiting for a tip.

I opened my wallet halfheartedly and handed him some bills with a sigh.

"That's it?" he complained **loudly**.

Everybody turned to look at us.

I didn't want to look bad in front of Petunia, so I handed him the entire wallet.

Then I collapsed in a chair while Petunia, Bugsy, and Benjamin went for a walk.

Oh, what a miserable vacation!

HE'S A MESS!

Lulled by the sound of the WAVES, I was about to drift off to sleep. But suddenly, three FRAIL voices woke me up.

"It's him, Gladys."

"Are you sure, Mitzi?"

"You ask him, Gertrude."

"Excuse me, aren't you Geronimo Stilton, the bigshot newspaper mouse?"

I opened my eyes.

Three old ladies stood over me.

"Um, yes, I'm Geronimo Stilton," I said.

"He's much better looking in photos, don't you agree, Mitzi?" the first mouse commented.

"Oh, definitely, Gertrude," the second mouse said. "Look at his fur. It's all knotted.

And what's with his eyes? Are they crossed? What do you think, Gladys?"

"He's a mess!" the third mouse announced.

I sighed. I felt a pounding headache coming on.

"Sorry to disappoint you," I said.

I was about to close my eyes again when one of the old ladies pulled out a HUGE stack of papers.

"Even though you're a mess, we still want your autograph. Can you sign one for each of us, and one for all our friends?" she asked.

I gulped.

If my eyes weren't crossed now, they would be by the time I finished signing all of those sheets. It would take me hours!

But what could I do? After all, I am a gentlemouse.

With a sigh, I bent my head and started signing.

Oh, what a miserable vacation!

I signed and signed and signed and signed . . .
I signed and signed and signed and signed . . .
I signed and signed and signed and signed . . .
I signed and signed and signed and signed . . .
I signed and signed and signed and signed . . .
I signed and signed and signed and signed . . .
I signed and signed and signed and signed . . .
I signed and signed and signed and signed . . .
I signed and signed and signed and signed . . .
I signed and signed and signed and signed . . .
I signed and signed and signed and signed . . .
I signed and signed and signed and signed . . .
I signed and signed and signed and signed . . .
I signed and signed and signed and signed . . .
I signed and signed and signed and signed . . .
I signed and signed and signed and signed . . .
I signed and signed and signed and signed . . .
I signed and signed and signed and signed . . .
I signed and signed and signed and signed . . .
I signed and signed and signed and signed . . .
I signed and signed and signed and signed . . .

Sigh . . .

HEY, UNCLE G!

After the busybodies left, I closed my eyes. Ah, at last — a little peace and quiet. The sun warmed my fur. And the sound of the ocean waves was so *relaxing*. I was about

Bonk!

to drift off when a beach ball **SMACKED** me in the snout.

Bonk!

"Hey, Uncle G! Guess what I've got?" Bugsy screeched, waving a **GIANT** book in my face. Before I could answer, she continued, "It's the *Encyclopedia of Jokes*!

And I'm going to read them all to you. Every **single** one!"

For the next hour, Bugsy forced me to listen to the most **RIDICULOUS** jokes ever. By the time she was done I thought my head would **EXPLODE**.

Oh, what a miserable vacation!

Bugsy Wugsy's Jokes

SHARK GAME

What musical game do sharks like playing the most?

Name that tuna.

DOWN AND OUT IN OCTOPUS HILLS

Where do you find a down and out octopus?

On Squid Row.

SEAWEED FOR HIRE

Where does seaweed look for a job?

In the Kelp Wanted ads.

OPERATION FISH

Which fish can perform operations?

A sturgeon.

WHAT'S THE DEAL?

Why couldn't the sailor play cards on his boat?

Because someone was always sitting on his deck.

"WEIGH" TO GO!

Why is it so easy to weigh fish?

Because fish have their own scales.

SAY WHAT?

What did the Pacific Ocean say to the Atlantic Ocean?

Nothing, it just waved.

By midafternoon, Petunia, Benjamin, and Bugsy decided to go check out the hotel's game room. But I wasn't budging. The thought of hanging out in a noisy game room with Bugsy made my head pound.

"Use the SUNBLOCK in the beach bag," Petunia said, waving good-bye.

I looked in the bag and found a bottle filled with a STICKY liquid.

1) I rubbed the liquid from the tip of my whiskers to the tip of my tail.

2) I fell asleep in the sun for hours.

3) I woke up with a horrible burn.

4) I tried to get up, but I tripped and fell.

5) I looked like a breaded mouse cutlet!

I read the bottle. SLIMY CHEDDAR STICKS!

It wasn't sunblock — it was **shampoo**!

Oh, what a miserable vacation!

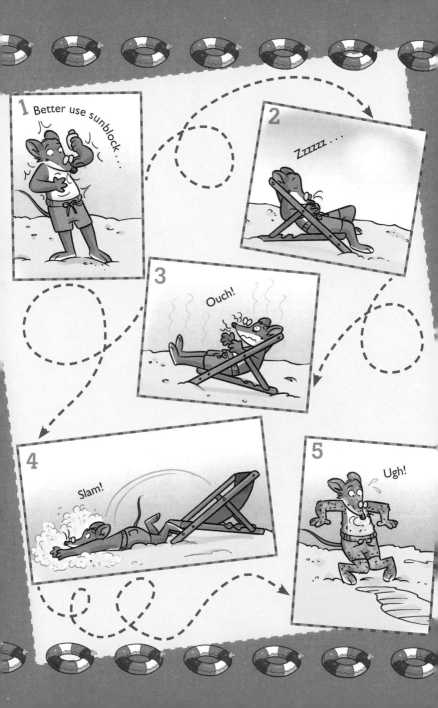

How Sad!

I decided to jump in the water to get the sand off me. As a young mouseling, I used to love **swimming** in the beautiful blue-green water.

I remembered fondly how . . .

Geronimo as a mouseling

...the clear waves TWINKLED in the sunlight...

...the **fresh** breeze smelled of salt...

...the seagulls flapped in the sky...

...and the whales LEAPED and

played on the horizon.

Now, ugly trash floated here and there in the waves. The air STUNK of smog, and there were no whales in sight.

How sad!

GET YOUR CAMERA!

I stuck a paw in the water. **Frozen** cheese puffs, it was **COLD**! I decided to skip the swim, but just then a wave knocked me over. It pulled me underwater.

I was tossed around . . .

AND AROUND... AND AROUND... AND AROUND...

AND AROUND... AND AROUND... AND AROUND...

AND AROUND... AND AROUND... AND AROUND...

As I struggled to get to the top, I lost my bathing suit in the **undertow**!

Holey cheese! **How humiliating!** What was I supposed to do?

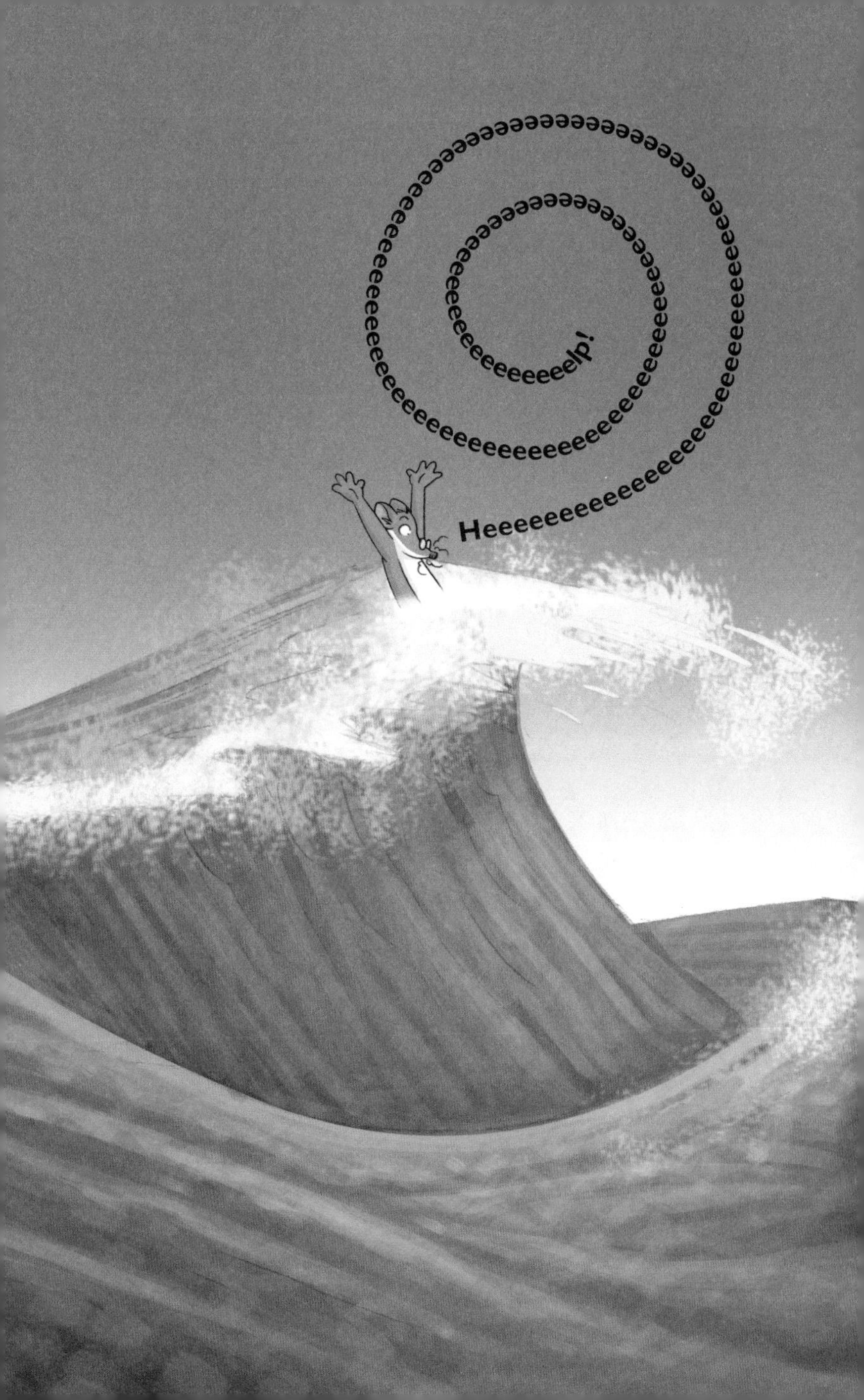

I thought and thought until at last I came up with a plan. I waited until the sun went down. Then I slipped out of the water. I found some seaweed that had washed up on the beach and wove it into a pair of swimming trunks. Then I SNUCK over to the hotel by going the back way, so no one would see me.

When I got there, I waited until the doorman was busy before I grabbed the key to my room.

Then I ran **up** the stairs, **DOWN** the hall, and **STRAIGHT** to my room.

But just as I was about to go in, I heard three **shrieks**.

I cringed. Then I slowly turned around.

It was the **three** busybodies from the beach!

"Do you see what he's wearing, Mitzi?" one said.

"It looks like *seaweed*," said another. "What do you think, Gladys?"

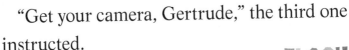

"Get your camera, Gertrude," the third one instructed.

Before I could protest, a bright **FLASH** went off.

I hung my head. How embarrassing!

Oh, what a miserable vacation!

SEAWEED SWIM TRUNKS!

The next day all the gossip magazines on Mouse Island showed a picture of me on the cover. Can you guess what I was wearing? Yup, I had on SEAWEED swim trunks!

Could things get any worse?

I went down to breakfast and there were the three busybodies.

I tried to crawl under a table, but they started shrieking.

"Look, everyone! There he is!" they shouted. "It's Geronimo Stilton! Where's your seaweed swimsuit?"

Oh, what a miserable vacation!

I was purple with embarrassment.

Petunia would never take me seriously

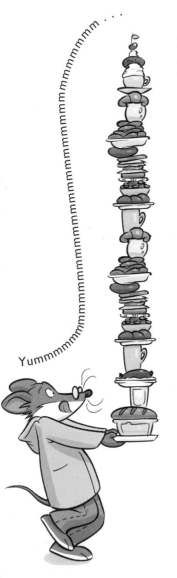

Yummmmmmmmmmmmmmmmmmmmmmmmmmmmmmmmm . . .

now. How could I tell her I liked her after this **DISASTER**?

I was so upset I hid under the buffet table. But then my stomach started to **rumble**. The smell of **HOT** cinnamon rolls, **jelly** doughnuts, and **cheese** Danish made my mouth water.

I couldn't stop myself. I popped up from under the table, grabbed a plate, and piled it **high** with all kinds of **delicious** breakfast foods. There were cheddar pancakes, waffles, mozzarella muffins, cheesy

crepes, bagels, and French toast.

While I was eating, I began to feel **better**. Maybe things weren't so bad after all. I tried to forget about my seaweed swimsuit and concentrate on something positive. Since it was our second-to-last day at the beach, I had booked tickets for us to go **WHALE WATCHING**. I couldn't wait.

I Was So Excited!

Right then, Petunia showed up. When she saw my breakfast plate, she **shook** her head.

"G, you ate too much," she scolded. "When you go on a boat, you can't **OVEREAT**."

It was too late. I was full to the brim.

A few minutes later, we boarded a **GLASS**-bottom boat. It was **amazing**! We could see the fish as if we were right in the water! The boat went out to sea so we could get a better look at some **WHALES**.

I WAS SO EXCITED!

Partly it was because we were going to see whales. But mostly it was because I had decided that as soon as we got out to open sea, I'd tell Petunia that I liked her.

My paws were sweaty . . .

My mouth was as dry as sand . . .

My whiskers trembled with nerves . . .

I was going to give Petunia a rose. And I had even made up a poem.

You are so smart, so kind, and so sweet,
Being with you is really a treat.
We have tons of fun when we're together,
Even if it's under gray stormy weather.
Your smile is like sunshine, your laughter like candy,
Your fur is still pretty even when it gets sandy.
So this poem is for you and I hope it's okay,
If I tell you I like you more each passing day!

To be sure I wouldn't forget it, I wrote the poem on the palm of my **paw**.

Finally, we got to the **high seas**. The waves pushed the boat **Up** and **down**.

Up and **down** . . . **Up** and **down** . . . **Up** and **down** !

Petunia was below in her cabin. As I stepped down the small ladder, I felt my head spinning **around, around, around, around**. . . .

It's because I'm so excited! I thought.

When I got to the cabin, I felt a *knot* in my stomach.

It's because I'm so excited! I thought.

My knees were becoming **mush**.

It's because I'm so excited! I thought.

Then, to my **HORROR**,

I realized something else was happening.

I wasn't excited. I was *seasick*!

My fur turned **green** as a cucumber. My stomach **lurched**.

Why hadn't I listened to Petunia's advice about overeating?

Oh, what a miserable vacation!

WHAT TO EAT AND NOT EAT WHEN YOU'RE AT SEA:

Before boarding, don't eat any heavy, fatty, or fried foods, as they're hard to digest. During the trip, it's better to eat a light meal, or snack on crackers, bread sticks, or just plain bread. Don't drink too much and avoid fizzy beverages. Also avoid fruit juices and acidic fruit like oranges, lemons, and grapefruits.

YOUR SMILE IS
SANDY . . .

By the time I found Petunia, my tongue was **hanging** out of my mouth and I was shaking like a leaf. I felt like a circus mouse about to fly out of a cannon.

I clutched the **rose** (and my stomach) and tried to recite my poem. But I was feeling so awful I couldn't get anything right.

"Your fur is **gray** . . . I mean, your smile is **sandy** . . . I mean, being with you is like *stormy* weather. . . ." I stammered. What a **DISASTER**!

Then I remembered I had written the poem down on my paw so I wouldn't forget it. But when I looked at my paw, the ink was all **SMEARED** with my sweat.

Meanwhile, Petunia was staring at me as if I had three tails.

"Is there something you wanted to tell me, G?" she asked.

I took a deep breath.

"Petunia . . ." I began.

But the NOISE of the boat's engine MUFFLED my words.

So I tried again. "Petunia . . ." I began.

But the boat started to ROCK under a passing wave.

"Petunia . . ." I cried, before I raced out of her cabin. "I'm seasick!"

IT'S A WHALE!

Up on deck I clung to the side of the boat. Everybody was staring at me, looking disgusted. I heard them murmuring among themselves.

"It's him again. The one with the teensy weensy seaweed suit."

"Yup, it figures."

"Did you see how he wolfed down the buffet?"

"Look how sick he is. HOW REVOLTING! It serves him right!"

Oh, what a miserable vacation!

Even though I was still feeling awful, I decided to join Petunia on deck. She was listening to the whales using a special

TEN STEPS OF SEASICKNESS

1 The sea is so beautiful!

2 Hmm . . . it's a little rocky!

3 Oops . . . it's really wobbly!

4 I feel a little weird. . . .

5 Yuck, I ate too much!

6 Ouch! Ouch! My stomach hurts!

7 be I'll feel better like this. . . .

8 Oh, no! I'm getting dizzy!

9 I don't think I can make it!

10 Heeeeeeeeeeeeeeeeeeeeeeeeeeeeeeeeeeeeeeeeeeeeeeeeeeeeeeeeeeeeeeeeeeeeelp!

HOW TO OBSERVE WHALES

Have you ever gone whale watching? It involves looking at whales in their natural habitat. In some places by the sea, with a little patience and luck, it's possible to see whales from the beach, or by taking a trip on a boat. However, it's important to never disturb the whales!

Whales make certain musical sounds that can travel underwater for several miles. They can be heard with a special instrument called a hydrophone.

Binocular

Camera

Headphones with recorder

Battery

The hydrophone is an instrument that discerns sounds underwater. It's made from a microphone, a battery, and headphones with a recorder.

The boat needs to move slowly and maintain a distance of at least 100 yards from the whales to not disturb them.

Microphone

instrument called a hydrophone. Suddenly, on the horizon, we saw something shoot a stream of water into the air. Then it splashed the water with loud flaps of its tail.

"Look, G!" Petunia shouted. "It's a whale! It's a whale!" She was so excited she jumped up and down, squeaking.

Normally I love Petunia's squeak, but today every time she squeaked, my head pounded and my stomach lurched.

She handed me the binoculars so I could see the whales better, but I was too weak to hold them. Oh, when would this boat ride end?

HOW TO IDENTIFY WHALES

THERE ARE SEVERAL KINDS OF WHALES. TO IDENTIFY THE MOST COMMON SPECIES, ONE NEEDS ONLY TO OBSERVE ITS DIMENSIONS AND SOME VERY PARTICULAR CHARACTERISTICS. LET'S IDENTIFY THEM TOGETHER!

1 If you see a whale with a large tail with an irregular shape and black and white coloring . . .

. . . if you see a whale with a low and stumpy fin on its back with a hump near its head . . .

2 If you see a whale with a wide, flat, slightly V-shaped tail . . .

. . . if you see a whale with a small, stumpy fin and a slightly round point on its back . . .

3 If you see a whale with a wide and triangular tail . . .

. . . if you see a whale with a triangular or rounded hump instead of a dorsal fin . . .

. . . if you see a whale blowing a dense and very visible jet as high as 9 feet . . .

. . . THEN YOU'RE SEEING A **1**

HUMPBACK WHALE!

. . . if you see a whale blowing a thin, vertical, column-like jet as high as 39 feet . . .

. . . THEN YOU'RE SEEING A **2**

BLUE WHALE!

. . . if you see a whale blowing a low, dense jet projected forward and slightly to the left . . .

. . . THEN YOU'RE SEEING A **3**

SPERM WHALE!

A MYSTERIOUS SHADOW IN THE NIGHT

We finally returned to shore. I was so happy to be on dry land!

After dinner, I asked Petunia to take a walk

on the beach with me.

I was looking forward to a nice peaceful stroll in the **moonlight**. But Bugsy insisted on tagging along. She dragged Benjamin with her.

We were only walking for a few minutes when we spotted a **MYSTERIOUS SHADOW** in the night.

Was it a shipwreck?

Or an alien **SPACESHIP**?

Or a mouse-eating sea monster?

Then I heard a sound: "Swisssshhhhh!"

A shower of seawater **DRENCHED** me from the tip of my nose to the tip of my tail.

INCREDIBLE!

It was a whale!

But what was a whale doing in the **middle** of the beach?

Swissshhhhh! Swisssshhhhh! Swisssshhhhh! Swisssshhhhh! Swisssshhhhh! Swisssshhhhh! Swisssshhhhh! Swisssshhhhh! Swisssshhhhh! Swisssshhhhh! Swisssshhhhh! Swisssshhhhh! Swisssshhhhh! Swisssshhhhh! Swisssshhhhh! Swisssshhhhh! Swisssshhhhh!

"She's probably sick, or lost her sense of direction," Petunia said. "We need to contact the marine authorities right away. They'll know how to get her back to the sea where she belongs."

Did I mention Petunia knows a lot about **ANIMALS** and **NATURE**?

BEACHING

Beaching is a natural phenomenon by which cetaceans (whales and dolphins) and also turtles get stuck on sandy beaches.

The reasons for this are varied: For example, the animal could be sick, or currents, tides, loss of direction, storms, and earthquakes could cause them to end up on the beach. Usually, beached cetaceans cannot return to sea by themselves.

Here are some ways to help them!

If you find a whale or a dolphin on the beach . . .

WHAT TO DO:

1. Immediately call the local authorities.
2. The authorities will know what experts to contact to help the whale in danger.
3. In the meantime, keep the skin of the whale wet.
4. If there is sun, shade the whale if possible so that its delicate skin doesn't burn.
5. Keep onlookers away.
6. If possible, keep the animal's tummy down, with its back facing up.

WHAT NOT TO DO:

1. Do not touch the animal (unless absolutely necessary).
2. Do not push or pull the tail or fins.
3. Do not put any sunblock lotion on the animal!
4. Don't cover the animal's blowhole. (Remember, the blowhole is the hole from which the spray exits, and how the whale breathes.)
5. Do not let any sand or water get into the blowhole.
6. Do not make any loud noise, and talk as little as possible so as not to frighten the whale.

Is It Still Breathing?

Petunia grabbed her cell phone and called for **help**. While she was squeaking, I studied the whale. It didn't look good.

Then I remembered something I had heard about whales. The whale's skin is super **delicate**. It needs to be kept **moist** at all times.

I grabbed Benjamin's beach pail and filled it up with **WATER**. I poured it over the whale. The kids and I took turns racing back and forth trying to **wet** down the whale with sea water.

But the whale was **ENORMOUSE**.

Slowly, its eyes closed.

It was no longer **SPRAYING**.

My heart felt like a stale lump of cheese.

"Uncle Geronimo, is it still breathing?" Benjamin gulped.

I wasn't sure. After all, this was the first whale I had ever seen up close and personal. "Let's hope for the best," I said. I CROSSED my whiskers for good luck.

Just as Petunia snapped her cell phone shut, a **moonbeam** lit up the whale.

We gasped.

How incredible!

It

was a

white

whale!

"Oh my gosh, G!" Petunia cried. "It's an extremely rare **white** humpback whale!"

HUMPBACK

The **humpback** is a baleen whale, one of the larger rorqual species. Adults range in length up to 52 feet, and can weigh up to 79,000 pounds. The humpback is a slow swimmer and feeds mostly on *krill** (little shellfish similar to small shrimp), and small fish (especially anchovies). To get its prey, it circles a school of fish and traps them in an air bubble net emitted from the blowhole that can be as large as 145 feet across.

It has a thin head with *knobs** . . .

. . . and is an acrobatic animal. When it surfaces, it can jump clear out of the water. This is called *breaching**.

The **dorsal fin** is low and hard, and the whale has a hump near its head.

Humpbacks use their massive **tail fins** to propel themselves through the water. They stick their tail out of the water and into the air, swing it around, and then slap it on the water's surface, making a loud sound. This is called *lobtailing**.

. . . Humpbacks have two **blowholes**, like all baleen whales.

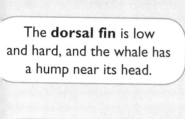

The humpback's scientific name is **Megaptera noveangliae**, *Megaptera* means "giant wing," and refers to the whales' long **front flippers**, characterized also by lumps along their edges.

* See the minidictionary on page 102.

Petunia explained that the whale was white because it was an albino. Albinos have no color to their skin because their body does not produce something called melanin.

"Remember Moby Dick, the white whale in Herman Melville's story? He was an albino sperm whale," Petunia added.

I nodded.

(Do you know **HERMAN MELVILLE**? He was an amazing writer of long ago.)

I was still thinking about Herman Melville when Benjamin suggested we name our whale **HOPE**.

"Oh, G, I hope Hope makes it," Petunia whispered, **SQUEEZING** my paw tightly.

I tried to agree but I could hardly breathe. Petunia's grip was killing me!

Did I mention she is an extremely **STRONG** mouse?

HERMAN MELVILLE

Herman Melville was born in New York in 1819. Left penniless by his father, he often worked as a sailor on the ocean. These trips inspired his first adventure novels. His greatest

Herman Melville

masterpiece, *Moby-Dick*, was published in 1851. The story tells of a voyage on the whaling ship *Pequod*, commanded by Captain Ahab. The crew on the ship hunt whales, specifically the enormous white whale called Moby Dick.

Herman Melville died in New York in 1891 at the age of 72.

(excerpt from *Moby-Dick*, Chapter 133)

"There she blows! — there she blows! A hump like a snow-hill! It is Moby Dick!"

Fired by the cry which seemed simultaneously taken up by the three look-outs, the men on deck rushed to the rigging to behold the famous whale they had so long been pursuing. Ahab had now gained his final perch, some feet above the other look-outs, Tashtego standing just beneath him on the cap of the top-gallant mast, so that the Indian's head was almost on a level with Ahab's heel. From this height the whale was now seen some mile or so ahead, at every roll of the sea revealing his high sparkling hump, and regularly jetting his silent spout into the air. To the credulous mariners it seemed the same silent spout they had so long ago beheld in the moonlit Atlantic and Indian Oceans.

Good-Bye, Hope!

Before long, the **RESCUE TEAM** arrived. Petunia's friend, **Dr. Tina Louise Cuddlefur** (nickname: Dr. TLC) was in charge.

She wore a WHITE lab coat, glasses, and a serious expression.

"You were right to try to keep the whale's

skin **WET**," she said after she examined Hope. "But now we need to give her some medicine and get her back to the sea as *quickly* as possible."

Petunia, Benjamin, Bugsy, and I sprang into action. We set up some **floodlights** on the beach so Dr. TLC and the other vets could see. Then we watched as the doctors gave her medicine and carefully wrapped her body in soaking wet towels.

At dawn, Dr. TLC decided Hope was strong enough to return to sea.

We helped fasten her to floaters tied by **STRONG** but **soft** ropes. The ends of the ropes were attached to a large tugboat. When the doctor gave the signal, we all began to pull.

The rope **dug** into my paws. My back

ACHED. My shoulders **BURNED**. I chewed my whiskers to keep from sobbing. After all, I didn't want to embarrass myself in front of Petunia.

As soon as she was in the open sea, Hope dove underwater, SPLASHING the surface with her tail as if waving good-bye.

"Good-bye, Hope!" we all shouted.

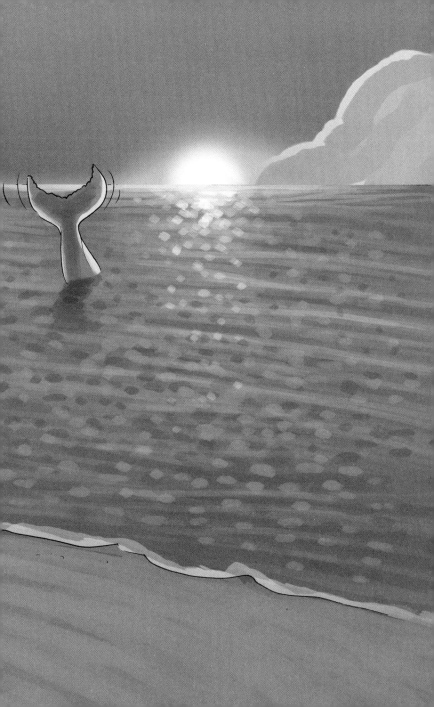

PROJECT SAVE THE WHITE WHALE

The next Monday I was back in my office in New Mouse City looking at pictures from my **vacation**. That's when I came up with a GREAT idea. I would publish a special edition of *The Rodent's Gazette* all about the Bay of Whales. I would write about the smoke and the factories. I would write about the **litter** on the beach and the **NOISY** traffic. And of course, I would write about the whales.

The next day, thousands of letters poured in. I couldn't believe how many rodents cared about the **Bay of Whales**. Petunia, Benjamin, and Bugsy helped me read the letters.

"I have an idea," said Petunia. "We could have *The Rodent's Gazette* collect signatures to have the Bay of Whales declared a **protected natural marine park**."

"That's a great idea," I said. "We can call it Project Save the White Whale."

The next day, I got all of my friends and family involved in the project. I asked my friend in **advertising** to help get the word out. I asked my *lawyer*

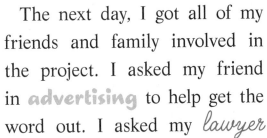

SIGNATURE COLLECTION

friend to give me advice on collecting the signatures. I asked my *baker* friend to pass out cheese treats to everyone waiting in line to sign the petition. I even asked my *aunt Sweetfur* to help answer the phones.

It was a **FABUMOUSE** success!

A month later we heard back

from the Mouse Island ENVIRONMENTAL PROTECTION AGENCY. They checked out our claims and decided the Bay of Whales was a precious treasure.

The bay was declared a Protected Marine Park.

ANYTHING IS POSSIBLE . . .

Before long, the bay was BUSTLING with activity.

Giant purifiers were installed to clean the dirty seawater. All of the garbage was picked up from the beach. And the factories that POLLUTED the air with their TOXIC fumes were shut down.

The center of the town at the Bay of Whales was closed to cars. And a small museum was built by the water, where visitors could view all kinds of MARINE LIFE.

Best of all, Miss Sweetcakes went back to running Whales and Tails by the Sea.

I was happy the bay was back to the way I remembered it when I was little.

I started taking vacations there again. As soon as I finished work, I headed down to the bay for the **weekend**. Soon all of my friends and family were joining me — my sister, Thea, my cousin Trap, and my friend Hercule Poirat.

Everyone *loved* the beaches and the whales and dolphins enjoyed the attention. They JUMPED and DOVE into the sea, waving their fins at the crowd.

One weekend, Petunia joined me. We had a great time watching the whales from a boat, partly because whales are so fascinating, and partly because I took seasickness pills before we left the dock.

I still haven't told Petunia that I *like* her. But someday I will. After all, if I can help save a white whale, ANYTHING is POSSIBLE!

What are YOU doing to help the environment?

You, too, can give a little or a lot to help save the planet!

Whales

Whales and dolphins are part of a large family of cetaceans. Cetaceans are mammals (just like humans) that live in water. They are marine mammals.

WHALES ARE NOT FISH

Whales, and cetaceans in general, look like fish because they have fins and a tail, but they are not! They do not breathe underwater. They breathe from nostrils called blowholes when they surface and inhale air into their lungs. For a long time, whales were called "fish with spouts."

A FEW NUMBERS . . .

Baleen whales are part of a group called "Mysticeti," the largest cetaceans on earth. The blue whale can reach 110 feet in length and can eat 5 tons of shrimp a day. Blue whales can weigh up to 150 tons.

INTERESTING FACTS

Did you know whales talk? They emit underwater sounds, with different pitches and frequencies, that they use to communicate with one another. Mother and calf, for example, can recognize one another through individual sounds called "signature whistles" that are different for each whale. The complex whale songs can be heard for miles under the water.

CETACEAN MINIDICTIONARY

Beaching: Natural phenomenon occurring with cetaceans and turtles when, for various reasons, they are washed ashore.

Blow or spout: Cloud of water and vapor sprayed by cetaceans as part of a whale's breathing process.

Cetacean: Marine mammal belonging to the cetacean family. Whales and dolphins are cetaceans.

Fluke: Flat horizontal tail of a cetacean.

Krill: Tiny shellfish similar to small shrimp. Whales and other cetaceans often feed on krill.

Knot/Knob: Bump-like, roundish swelling along the rim of the fins and heads of some cetaceans.

Pectoral flipper: Cetacean forelimb that's shaped like a spatula.

Whale watching: Observing cetaceans in their natural habitat — the sea.

CETACEAN ACTIVITIES

BREACHING: This is a complete (or almost complete) flip of the cetacean's body out of the water.

FLUKING: When a cetacean raises its tail out of the water as it begins a dive.

FLIPPER-SLAPPING: When a cetacean energetically raises and slaps its pectoral fin on the water's surface.

LOBTAILING: A cetacean activity in which the animal sticks its tail out of the water and into the air, swings it around, and then slaps it on the water's surface while the rest of the body stays immersed in water.

On the return trip from the Bay of Whales, Petunia taught us an awesome game. Benjamin and Bugsy discovered that they had learned quite a lot about whales, thanks to this fabumouse adventure. You can play this game, too!

Did You See a Whale in the Middle of the Sea?

This is a fun game but it requires a lot of concentration and good memory. You need at least two players. The first player says, "I saw a whale in the middle of the sea . . ." and the second player repeats what the first player said and adds a phrase that can then be added to by another person. The third player repeats the entire sentence and adds a few more words, and so on. For example:

First person: "I saw a whale in the middle of the sea . . ."

Second person: "I saw a whale in the middle of the sea and it had a long fin . . ."

Third person: "I saw a whale in the middle of the sea and it had a long fin and it was white . . ."

Whoever makes a mistake in remembering the entire sentence is out of the game. The winner is the one that lasts the longest.

How ecologically friendly are you?

Take this quiz to see if you know the best way to act to help the environment!

1 What should you do with a magazine you don't want anymore?

a) Throw it in a recycling bin.
b) Throw it on the ground.
c) Throw it in a Dumpster.

2 What's the most ecologically friendly way to cool your house down in the summer?

a) Turn the air conditioner on full blast.
b) Install a ceiling fan that consumes little energy but cools the air.
c) Keep the refrigerator door open, so at least it's cool in the kitchen!

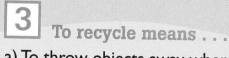

3 To recycle means . . .

a) To throw objects away when they're not in use or no longer needed.

b) To reuse objects to reduce the consumption of raw materials and minimize pollution

c) To hide objects you no longer need in your basement.

4 How should you clean up after a party?

a) Throw the glass bottles, plastic plates and cups, napkins, and leftover food all into one big trash bag.

b) Hide everything under the bed!

c) Sort the trash according to type, putting glass, paper, plastics, and food leftovers in separate containers according to your city's recycling instructions.

Match the name!

On the following page are drawings of
many different sea creatures. Match up
the creatures with their names using
the corresponding numbers!

HUMPBACK WHALE ◯

OCTOPUS ◯

BLUE WHALE ◯

SHARK ◯

SPERM WHALE ◯

SWORDFISH ◯

LOBSTER ◯

SEAHORSE ◯

DOLPHIN ◯

CRAB ◯

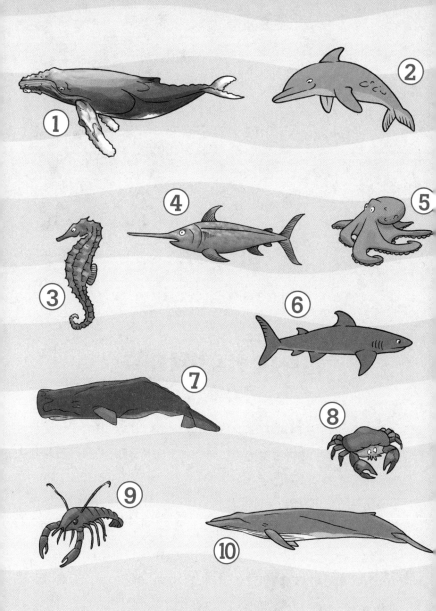

Want to read my next adventure?
I can't wait to tell you all about it!

THE HAUNTED CASTLE

I was just minding my business at home when I got a telephone call. It was my uncle Samuel S. Stingysnout, inviting the whole Stilton family to creepy, faraway Penny Pincher Castle for a big surprise. Moldy mozzarella! I'm not much of a traveling mouse, and I hate surprises. But Thea, Trap, and Benjamin were going, so I couldn't say no. I could tell this was going to be one super-spooky trip!

And don't miss any of my other fabumouse adventures!

#1 LOST TREASURE OF THE EMERALD EYE

#2 THE CURSE OF THE CHEESE PYRAMID

#3 CAT AND MOUSE IN A HAUNTED HOUSE

#4 I'M TOO FOND OF MY FUR!

#5 FOUR MICE DEEP IN THE JUNGLE

#6 PAWS OFF, CHEDDARFACE!

#7 RED PIZZAS FOR A BLUE COUNT

#8 ATTACK OF THE BANDIT CATS

#9 A FABUMOUSE VACATION FOR GERONIMO

#10 ALL BECAUSE OF A CUP OF COFFEE

#11 IT'S HALLOWEEN, YOU 'FRAIDY MOUSE!

#12 MERRY CHRISTMAS, GERONIMO!

#13 THE PHANTOM OF THE SUBWAY

#14 THE TEMPLE OF THE RUBY OF FIRE

#15 THE MONA MOUSA CODE

#16 A CHEESE-COLORED CAMPER

#17 WATCH YOUR WHISKERS, STILTON!

#18 SHIPWRECK ON THE PIRATE ISLANDS

#19 MY NAME IS STILTON, GERONIMO STILTO

#20 SURF'S UP, GERONIMO!

#21 THE WILD, WILD WEST

#22 THE SECRET OF CACKLEFUR CASTLE

A CHRISTMAS TALE

#23 VALENTINE'S DAY DISASTER

#24 FIELD TRIP TO NIAGARA FALLS

#25 THE SEARCH FOR SUNKEN TREASURE

#26 THE MUMMY WITH NO NAME

#27 THE CHRISTMAS TOY FACTORY

#28 WEDDING CRASHER

#29 DOWN AND OUT DOWN UNDER

#30 THE MOUSE ISLAND MARATHO

#31 THE MYSTERIOUS CHEESE THIEF

CHRISTMAS CATASTROPHE

#32 VALLEY OF THE GIANT SKELETONS

#33 GERONIMO AND THE GOLD MEDAL MYSTERY

#34 GERONIMO STILTON, SECRET AGENT

#35 A VERY MERRY CHRISTMAS

#36 GERONIMO'S VALENTINE

#37 THE RACE ACROSS AMERICA

#38 A FABUMOUSE SCHOOL ADVENTURE

#39 SINGING SENSATION

#40 THE KARATE MOUSE

#41 MIGHTY MOUNT KILIMANJARO

#42 THE PECULIAR PUMPKIN THIEF

#43 I'M NOT A SUPERMOUSE!

#44 THE GIANT DIAMOND ROBBERY

Coming soon!

#46 THE HAUNTED CASTLE

Don't miss these very special editions!

THE KINGDOM OF FANTASY

THE QUEST FOR PARADISE:
THE RETURN TO THE KINGDOM OF FANTASY

Listen to a Double Dose of Geronimo's "Fabumouse" Adventures on Audio!

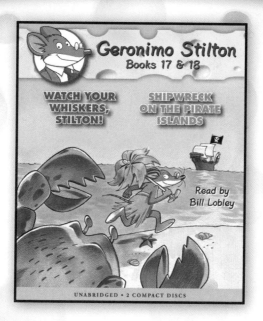

MORE 2-AUDIOBOOK PACKS AVAILABLE NOW:

WRITTEN BY *Geronimo Stilton*   READ BY *Bill Lobley*

If you like my brother's books,
check out the next adventure
of the Thea Sisters!

THEA STILTON AND
THE STAR CASTAWAYS

A professor at Mouseford Academy is organizing a trip to outer space, and the Thea Sisters are invited. The mouselings are headed on a fabumouse mission . . . to the moon! After much preparation, the mice blast off. But when they arrive at their lunar vacation spot, things start to go wrong, including spaceship wrecks and rebellious robots. Can the Thea Sisters save the day? Find out in an adventure that's out of this world!

Be sure to check out these other exciting Thea Sisters adventures:

**THEA STILTON
AND THE
DRAGON'S CODE**

**THEA STILTON
AND THE
MOUNTAIN OF FIRE**

**THEA STILTON
AND THE GHOST OF
THE SHIPWRECK**

**THEA STILTON
AND THE
SECRET CITY**

**THEA STILTON
AND THE MYSTERY
IN PARIS**

**THEA STILTON
AND THE
CHERRY BLOSSOM
ADVENTURE**

ABOUT THE AUTHOR

Born in New Mouse City, Mouse Island, **GERONIMO STILTON** is Rattus Emeritus of Mousomorphic Literature and of Neo-Ratonic Comparative Philosophy. For the past twenty years, he has been running *The Rodent's Gazette*, New Mouse City's most widely read daily newspaper.

Stilton was awarded the Ratitzer Prize for his scoops on *The Curse of the Cheese Pyramid* and *The Search for Sunken Treasure*. He has also received the Andersen 2000 Prize for Personality of the Year. One of his bestsellers won the 2002 eBook Award for world's best ratlings' electronic book. His works have been published all over the globe.

In his spare time, Mr. Stilton collects antique cheese rinds and plays golf. But what he most enjoys is telling stories to his nephew Benjamin.

1. Main entrance
2. Printing presses (where the books and newspaper are printed)
3. Accounts department
4. Editorial room (where the editors, illustrators, and designers work)
5. Geronimo Stilton's office
6. Helicopter landing pad

THE RODENT'S GAZETTE

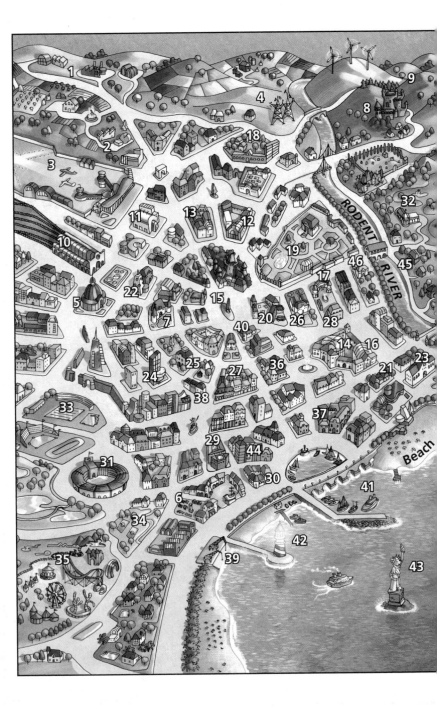

Map of New Mouse City

1. Industrial Zone
2. Cheese Factories
3. Angorat International Airport
4. WRAT Radio and Television Station
5. Cheese Market
6. Fish Market
7. Town Hall
8. Snotnose Castle
9. The Seven Hills of Mouse Island
10. Mouse Central Station
11. Trade Center
12. Movie Theater
13. Gym
14. Catnegie Hall
15. Singing Stone Plaza
16. The Gouda Theater
17. Grand Hotel
18. Mouse General Hospital
19. Botanical Gardens
20. Cheap Junk for Less (Trap's store)
21. Parking Lot
22. Mouseum of Modern Art
23. University and Library
24. *The Daily Rat*
25. *The Rodent's Gazette*
26. Trap's House
27. Fashion District
28. The Mouse House Restaurant
29. Environmental Protection Center
30. Harbor Office
31. Mousidon Square Garden
32. Golf Course
33. Swimming Pool
34. Blushing Meadow Tennis Courts
35. Curlyfur Island Amusement Park
36. Geronimo's House
37. New Mouse City Historic District
38. Public Library
39. Shipyard
40. Thea's House
41. New Mouse Harbor
42. Luna Lighthouse
43. The Statue of Liberty

Brigand's Isle

This way to the Rodent Straits

Tomcat Island

Pirate Ship of Cats

Hamster Islands

Coral Reefs

Blue Dolphin Bay

Cat's Claw Bay

Panther Archipelago

Swissville

This way to the Mousific Ocean

Stray Cat Harbor

Cheddarton

Mouseport

This way to the Ratlantic Ocean

San Mouscisco

New Mouse City

Mousefort Beach

Furflung Island

N
W   E
S

MOUSE ISLAND

This way to the Sea of Mice

Map of Mouse Island

1. Big Ice Lake
2. Frozen Fur Peak
3. Slipperyslopes Glacier
4. Coldcreeps Peak
5. Ratzikistan
6. Transratania
7. Mount Vamp
8. Roastedrat Volcano
9. Brimstone Lake
10. Poopedcat Pass
11. Stinko Peak
12. Dark Forest
13. Vain Vampires Valley
14. Goose Bumps Gorge
15. The Shadow Line Pass
16. Penny Pincher Castle
17. Nature Reserve Park
18. Las Ratayas Marinas
19. Fossil Forest
20. Lake Lake
21. Lake Lakelake
22. Lake Lakelakelake
23. Cheddar Crag
24. Cannycat Castle
25. Valley of the Giant Sequoia
26. Cheddar Springs
27. Sulfurous Swamp
28. Old Reliable Geyser
29. Vole Vale
30. Ravingrat Ravine
31. Gnat Marshes
32. Munster Highlands
33. Mousehara Desert
34. Oasis of the Sweaty Camel
35. Cabbagehead Hill
36. Rattytrap Jungle
37. Rio Mosquito

Dear mouse friends,
Thanks for reading, and farewell
till the next book.
It'll be another whisker-licking-good
adventure, and that's a promise!

Geronimo Stilton